SPACKS STREET

JOHNS HOPKINS: POETRY AND FICTION

John T. Irwin, general editor

SPACKS STREET

New & Selected Poems

BARRY SPACKS

The Johns Hopkins University Press
Baltimore & London

This book has been brought to publication with the generous assistance of the G. Harry Pouder Fund and the Albert Dowling Trust.

See p. 111 for permission notices
Copyright © 1982 by The Johns Hopkins University Press
Printed in the United States of America

The Johns Hopkins University Press, Baltimore, Maryland 21218
The Johns Hopkins Press Ltd., London

LIBRARY OF CONGRESS CATALOGING IN PUBLICATION DATA

Spacks, Barry.
    Spacks Street.

    (Johns Hopkins, poetry and fiction)
    I. Title.   II. Series.
PS3569.P33A6   1982   811'.54   82–15377
ISBN 0–8018–2890–2   AACR2
ISBN 0–8018–2892–9 (pbk.)

FOR KIMBERLEY
it changes

I suggest that you write with colored ink
what we were taught by K'ung fu-tzu:
Each of us is meant to rescue the world.

Evan S. Connell, *Points for a Compass Rose*

CONTENTS

V

NEW POEMS

SPACKS STREET

I
From
THE
COMPANY
OF CHILDREN

BLIND IN HIS SORROW

Blind in his sorrow and his fitful joy
he travels through the tangled wood of self
while she moves on beside him, meadow-sweet.

He blunders in the dark, afraid to see
how always she, beside him and before
makes everywhere a clearing; everywhere.

He stands upon his shadow's shrunken noon,
and if he'd take one step he'd come into
her love, that waits for him, a summer field.

FRESHMEN

My freshmen
settle in. Achilles
sulks; Pascal consults
his watch; and true
Cordelia—with her just-washed hair,

stern-hearted princess, ready to defend
the meticulous garden of truths in her highschool notebook—
uncaps her ballpoint pen.
And the corridors drum:
give us a flourish, flourescence of light, for the teachers come,

green and seasoned, bearers
of the Word, who differ
like its letters; there are some
so wise their eyes
are birdbites; one,

a mad, grinning gent with a golden tooth, God knows
he might be Pan, or the sub-
custodian; another
is a walking podium, dense
with his mystery—high

priests and attachés
of the ministry; kindly
old women, like unfashionable watering places;
and the assuming young, rolled tight as a City
umbrella;

thought-salesmen with samples cases,
and saints upon whom
merely to gaze is like Sunday—
their rapt, bright,
cat-licked faces!

4

And the freshmen wait;
wait bristling, acned, glowing like a brand,
or easy, chatting, munching, muscles lax,
each in his chosen corner, and in each
a chosen corner.

Full of certainties and reasons,
or uncertainties and reasons,
full of reasons as a conch contains the sea,
they wait; for the term's first bell;
for another mismatched wrestle through the year;

for a teacher who's religious in his art,
a wizard of a sort, to call the role
and from mere names
cause people
to appear.

The best look like the swinging door
to the Opera just before
the Marx Brothers break through.
The worst—debased,
on the back row,

as far as one can go
from speech—
are walls where childish scribbling's been erased;
are stones
to teach.

And I am paid to ask them questions:
Dare man proceed by need alone?
Did Esau like
his pottage?
Is any heart in order after Belsen?

And when one stops to think, I'll catch his heel,
put scissors to him, excavate his chest!
Watch, freshmen, for my words about the past
can make you turn your back. I wait to throw,
most foul, most foul, the future in your face.

EXERCISES

1 The Rose

Take a rose, a nominal rose,
in the mind's hand.
Do not lip it, or smell it,
but as the waves of a new thought rise
throw it, your rose,
and see it glide.
Now attempt
to prevent
its return
on the tide.

2 The Onion

A large, lusty one.
Strip it, make it young again,
and with the tip of the tongue,
or the pale inside of the arm,
or with the nose or the chin
deal with its smoothness, its curving
skin within skin.

Now cut it,
though you weep,
and fit it
back together.
Have you lost the wrapper?
Will the wound knit? will it heal?
There is no need
to repeat this exercise.

3 The Egg

> Having embraced yourself
>   in the fetal position,
>   you are the yellow,
>   the air is the white,
>   the house is the shell.
>
> What cracks the house?
>   What strains the air
>   to get at you?
>   It is the world.
>   Peck its hand!

THE WORLD AS A VISION
OF THE UNITY IN FLESH

Every Paris in the morning
When the mist is on the street
All the lovers fall to dreaming
Nose to nose and feet to feet,
Through the small-talk of the dawning
Like one body in their heat.

While the faithful dogs are yawning,
While the suicides are scheming,
All the lovers fall to dreaming
In this clearinghouse of woes;
All the lovers fall to dreaming
And their dreams are bittersweet;

All the lovers fall to dreaming
And they dream their dreams of those
Lying under clumsy covers
Close beside their newer lovers,
Who are dreaming dreams of others,
Feet to feet, and nose to nose.

THE COMPANY OF CHILDREN
for James Baker Hall

Desire may soar
from the valleys weightlessly
as in those nature films at school
where insects swell to premature old age
or sudden trees
surge up from seed to fruit
burning with power.

But the world, at its own good speed,
is tugged by oxen.

A house will not rise at a word;
its rafters will not lie patient in mid-air,
but must be muscled there;
struck humble.

The builder drives
his sharp axe in the wood,
across the natural fall
of speech and light.

To raise a house he leaves
dream-flight, and all thought of ease,
of instant mastery
of talents, instruments:
the hope that leaps
for a glimpse of the Garden.

And leaves the company of children:
of those who'd prove by crashing into trees
that forests are against them;
of those who'd have the Muse
—unwooed, ripe, incoherent girl—
fall in their laps with the smell
of bitten apples.

A house is raised
as one would go to mount a hill,
growing smaller as the hill
grows taller as he nears, until,
upon it,
fixed foot and quest foot, the hill
disappears; becomes
a topless tower; becomes
forever.

When at the top he stands, well pleased,
stands high with himself, he stands amazed:
the hill is smaller,
for he is taller
by a hill.

He builds his house,
and then returns
to the company
of children.

THREE SONGS
FOR MY DAUGHTER

1

Simply as the world is turning
Toward the ashes and the fuel,
Toward the secret of the burning
Simply as the world is turning
Children cross the road to school.

Many come to less by growing
Once the autumn's courses start.
Daughter, in the place you're going
Many come to less by growing,
Losing what they've had by heart.

Simply as the world is turning,
Scholar hand in hand with fool,
To a learning and unlearning
Simply as the world is turning
Children cross the road to school.

2

Child, where we stand
Is quicksand.

This venerable crust
Dust.

Move bravely on,
As if there were watchers.

3

Daughter, you will reach a twilight
Clear as joy: a summer evening
When the small bells ring and fingers
Stir within too swift for meaning.
Take the hand of your beloved;
In the bell of stillness gathered
Time will seem to pause for you.
Dear passenger: just so, so still
With us, until the rhyme for darkness
Booms—booms as if the feathers
Of all scattered birds were falling.
Night comes. Our voices, pounding,
Are the bells
That will your love.

THE OUTRAGEOUSLY BLESSED

The gods would have us chastened through confusion,
so those who tempt the skies' outrage are blessed.
Though Zeus might be a cupboy for the thanks he gets
from these,
the pretty boys who'd fall asleep
disputing with slow Socrates,
they're still the ones who catch the key equations
and laugh to straw the schoolmen and the schools;
they win the game by changing all the rules.

Small comfort for the sane, who do their best,
to find we cherish maddening exceptions:
. the lines that need not scan; the gulfs in nature;
the odds and irritants our cosmic oyster
cannot digest
as the pearl grows precious
in its queer success.

MY CLOTHES

Poor spineless things, the clothes I've shed
in hopes of the essential bed
of love. Like chastened dogs they wait
to be forgiven, stroked, pulled straight.
I lift them to the light, all holes
and patches, all the outworn roles,
the Dandy's musty ornaments,
the Lover's, and the Malcontent's.
The day seeks like a wind its form;
my clothes have kept me from the storm.
From age to age though I emerge
from cloying silks or common serge
my mere limbs stutter in the sun;
outside the cave, I come undone.
O, voices in your nakedness,
great dreamers in your skins or less,
make golden ages fill my mind
where ease leaves agony behind
and passion, all her raiment gone,
is beautiful with nothing on.

BIRTHDAY

Don't mention the rocks, the blocks from the quarries, the boulders . . .
I've work that is heavy enough in the dust of the gravel.
Far off in the distance they heave a few Alps on their shoulders.
I shudder, and bend my back low, and search with my tweezers.

More wise than my child when a wave leaps the moat of her castle,
I clear a new space, I sift through the thousands of pieces.
In shade from my arching body my fingers rustle,
And out where it's simple they lever the slab of Australia.

I laid out some stones, half-inches that looked like each other,
And rose, and stumbled, and scattered the ends of my labor.
How did it fit? how did it all fit together?
Behind me the children are digging a hole to China.

RECOMMENDATIONS

This is a good fellow
   who knows what he may do?
He is most excited, he is walking
   the walls of himself
on tiptoe. Give him
   a prize.

And this one is steady;
   it is clear that he is breathing;
he will never kill any number
   of old ladies, nor harrow
hell. Give him
   a prize.

AN EMBLEM OF TWO FOXES

Simply to breathe
can make him bleed,
the fox whose leg
is trapped, whose will
awaits the kill.
Why should he flail?
Moving hurts,
so he lies still.

Around him walks
a prouder fox,
his severed leg
a homily
on going free,
as if to say
it hurts, it hurts
either way.

THE CHANGING

Your kiss has made my mouth as smooth as light.
Made it your mouth, my face your face I wear,
your body on me that I can't wipe off:
like the glow of a daffodil
it echoes from my skin.

I am no deeply brighter now,
no stronger than I've ever been.
This newness on my lips can't heal your eyes.
And yet you gaze; you touch me like Miranda;
you touch me, and we shine.

Oh, but our bodies take such sweetness on!
Meeting, they barter, children jealous of the other's gift.
Changing, our bodies are like children,
blind children in their mother's house,
who know their way.

DAY FULL OF GULLS

Slow as the tide, a lifeguard smooths
his gritty girl, and seagulls stand,
and the shadows of clouds appear like pools,
and the waves fall back on themselves like sleep.

Day full of gulls, a storm of gulls,
wheel within wheel of caw and sweep,
never seeing enough of them,
how they tilt the air, and glide, and ebb.

At noon in the surf some raucous boys
made them scream like themselves, wings batting bodies,
vicious for lumps of last week's bread.
Day full of gulls. A storm of gulls.

Now women cast out evening crusts
like a sowing of love, and fathers aim
bits plucked like cake crumbs from the loaf,
to be snapped in mid-air with stern elegance.

A girl in the drift of the sea edge leans
on tiptoe, skirts held up. A gull
ends flight, like an indrawn breath,
on the small of his shadow.

AT 35

Father, what would you make of me? I wear your face.
I hear my cough and think the worms have sent you home.
Here at my table in my insubstantial house,
your myth of hope,
the piece of man you left,
I live your death
stroke for stroke.

There are no vows you did not keep I will not break.
I leave no darkness unacknowledged for your sake.
You are the school I teach. The course I take.
I move toward age, and you become my son.
Along the path ahead
you lift aside
the branches.

II
From
SOMETHING
HUMAN

THE ABSTRACT NOTION OF BOSTON, GATHERING DUST

for L. E. Sissman

Somewhere, among the scrimshaw and the bric-a-brac,
in the head of an old sailor, or in the thought
of a spinster tart as rust
lies the Abstract Notion of Boston, gathering dust.

I wasn't born to know this notion, but there must
still be a beanpot in it, and a ban on lust,
and Henry James and William James and Alice James
saying sentences to each other;

and one cold pot of harbor brewing
revolutionary tea;
and lawyers four abreast up Tremont
out for lunch, or equity,

footing it, doing it bostonly,
with hard coin reading In God we trust,
and a hint of antique musketry
in the flintlock chins of the upper crust.

O primly vulgar, practical city,
where lovers sail in a nutty swanboat
pair behind pair on a proper pond
and coo in a spinsterish, sailoresque accent;

O city of which all aunts are fond:
peacetroops marching on the Common;
leafsmoke scent in the Public Garden;
endless sound of Henry...William...

THE VIREO

for Virginia Prettyman

A girl stood, in the legendary light
of childhood, in Carolina, beside her father when he killed
a blacksnake in a tree
too high for either man or girl
to climb.
But snakes are climbers:
no height will keep them from
the eggs and young
of the "swinging birds," called so for their branch-hung
nests: the Vireo, whose name's source
remains mysterious.
Some call it
greenfinch: greenlet.
It was not
that her father shot the snake, for she'd expect
that of her father.
Nor that it fell
forty feet, a wheeling
coil.
But that a fledgling
flew from its mouth as it died:
arced up the full light's course
of her cry: a saved bird, a vaulter
from the dark
that bent its bones and gummed
its wool of feathers: O
greenfinch: greenlet: fly,
fly from the darkness, swinging bird.
Fly from that narrow mouth
as evening settles
among the oaks.

THE STROLLING CROW

for Bob Brill

1

Clumping along down the college path
like a proper man on a morning stroll
comes a cocky crow, as wide a crow
and tall and sleek and true a crow
as you'd ever see.

As nice a crow as I'll ever be.

I didn't expect to meet a crow
in just that way.
Pompous crow: pushy crow:
sharp and fat as a muscle-flex.
Left-step out, peck-glance, step right:
humorous crow: neighborly crow:
focus of light. Disinterested light.

But goodness knows, the cause of the crow's
strange strolling here
is clear as clear:

a crow can't hover
in the empty air
forever.

2

Crows on the highway, nailing down
a sometime rabbit.
Crows on the housetops. Crows on the lawn.
Beaks rivet.

Kin to vulture, raven, kite.
But crows are gayer.
This strolling crow, he passes like
an overseer.

Who'd expect a crow so wise
he'd nod? Implausible.
Come strolling crow, crow civilized,
anything's possible!

3

I'll take a crow for my emblem beast
in the game we play, "Reveal Your Soul,"
at faculty parties. Even though
the Grand Massif, moustached and piped,
who teaches history—man you'd think
would act the lion—speaks
Gazelle,
few'd choose a crow. Not even though
our loveliest lady's known to pick
pike in the lake, and once a snake
—she was tired that night, she was feeling like a saint;
she was dreaming of the sun on her saurian back—

but a *crow?*

4

That's me, that's me, purebred crow,
black as a splinter of anthracite coal,
bumpy old umbrella in a fumbly wind,
hard without if soft within;
sure and clean as a painted skull,
and shiny as a pocket comb:
bothered by a stuffed shirt:
awkward as a torn sheet
flopping on the laundry line—
rinsowhite turned insideout—

an honest creature:
rapacious in my nature:
formal dress: an agile eye:
clumping down the college path,
glancing right, glancing left:

what bird he'd be may mean the life
or the death of a man. Old crow,
pass on!

SHAVING

By undergrowth severely overgrown,
I've dulled 5000 Blue Blades, more or less,
Moved half a ton of lathered wilderness,
And still can't call this daily field my own.
I wonder does my brother Sisyphus
At least build muscle, shoving at his stone?

Sharp government may keep the crop in check,
But something wants to fur me like King Kong;
So as I shave the stubble's creeping back:
I turn the other cheek, to right the wrong,
And humble every hair, though not for long;
Till death can beard me, like a maniac.

Down, wantons, down! I'll cut you to the quick.
Mown close, I'd like to come on debonair.
Long years may weed out bristling rhetoric,
Intenser light leap up from trimmer wick,
And darker impulse yield to fasts, and prayer...
And still you rise again, my hopeful hair.

THE VET OF OUR DREAMS

*The younger bull may now try to take over as paramount
commander of the herd, but if he does, the veterinarian will saw his
antlers off, too.—New York Times*

Poor bull, you sort of lost your head
and took the whole elk herd to bed,
all for one and one for all.
For this, your antlers had to fall.
The vet who guards the neighborhood
removed them for the grouply good.
Your wild life-style caused too much fuss
among the more monogamous
who find, for better or for worse,
the horny bull a civic curse,
and now will straightway call the vet
as soon as youngsters start a set;
the vet of our dreams, whose trusty saw
creates one nation, under law.

THEMES ON LOVE

Grading themes on love at MIT,
one-man Symposium at 3
A.M., across the court I saw a light;
another office-holder working late.
While Plato on a silver pillow rode
above the waves of pre-sophistic prose,
I jotted teacher's notions that were not
as brave as our two lamps against the glut
of dawn. But when I clicked mine off
his too at once was gone: had been
my echo in a distant sheen
of glass: had been my own, and I
was lonely then, and wrote
these English words.

EMBLEMS FOR LOVERS

1

As one awaits a friend
who walks the path more slowly,
body, pause awhile
and wait for love.

2

"Love is a certain
inborn suffering,"
Andreas Capellanus said.
Though some would take it for a plaything,
or elegance of thought,
dumb as the tongue that knows no art
it must be fed.
It is the Basic English of the heart.
It is the crazy zoo beneath the skin.
The ape who shakes the bars through which he's staring.
The squirrel who blurs the body-wheel she's in.

3

Caged without bars, see two polar bears
on their split-level, concrete slab-of-the-moon.
One frolics alone in the pool, a charmer,
a seven-foot otter; one sways in woe,
his shabby back all knobbed with sores,
cobbles through last week's snow. Couples
grow pensive, here as at any zoo:
too much has been made in their image. The bears,
are they living emblems of Me and You?
of Us and Them? of Now and Then?
and what in the world did we used to do
for each other? Flamingos with scholar's eyes

fish troubled waters, while parrots rage;
a parakeet chatters; an eagle stares;
and the couples gaze
at the polar bears.

4

We are taking place in loneliness
like sounds
in silence.

I am empty, love.
I am a drum
for your hand.

SONGS FROM A COOK BOOK

(after instructions in *Mastering the Art of
French Cooking,* by Beck, Bertholle, and Child)

Spread the leaves apart, removing in one piece
the center cone.
Scrape off with a spoon
the choke, or hairy growth upon
the heart.

Or clear the whitish surface
with a knife held firmly;
rotate slowly;
and drop them as you finish
in acidulated water.

Choose the largest, the greenest
you can find.
Or allow for two
for each, preparing
one at a time.

•

This is the most convenient way
when the bird's to be readied to bear pâté:
    continue cutting against the bone
    and all will turn out as it should.

Stop, you must be careful here:
dangling legs and wings appear.
    Continue cutting against the bone
    and all will turn out as it should.

The skin is thin and easily split;
how in the world to make sense of it?
    Continue cutting against the bone
    and all will turn out as it should.

•

Open-faced Tarts are easy to make
but give them room, for they puff as they bake
and cooled they sink, collapsed on their backs;
but even cold they're tasty snacks,
    Open-faced Tarts.

Open-faced Tarts, they lend themselves,
supported solely by their shells,
to varied arrangements. Reheatable; quick;
nice to take along on a picnic,
    Open-faced Tarts.

•

If you were living in France you would buy
oval potatoes, two inches long,
with yellowish flesh:
pommes de terre de Hollande.

You would peel them smoothly to let them roll
and pat them thoroughly dry in a towel—
and eat them thoughtfully, sautéed whole—
if you were living in France.

MR. BERRYMAN'S READING

When Henry count his lumps at local U.
one row before me smellin happy sats
two muddle-agers, backheads crisp and nice.
They listen. Henry breathe; begins; begats
some question as to wherefore, namely who
he at with? Says, "they Mammoths in this ice?"

Well, Henry. Gruff an Scrappy. Gifty chap.
It cost him dear, this flaying out his mind;
and mainly seem he sort of miss mankind,
miss having-funs and swinkin how he sweve.
It weight me wif a tear to hear his hap.
The glads he sings, they wit me where I live.

But ah, come poet-chat, he playing rough.
High Henry diggeth not us audience—
but hunks: forked carnivores. He peers to guess
they been some mislay in the power-puff,
and he who get enough, will that one stand? and
all at once the couple upahead, they hand in hand—

the lady's squeeze the gent's, you understand—
she look toward ribby-like as if to state
"Oh, done I did you in, as Reader intimate?"
Yes, elsewheres and in manycase the females
checkin out their would-be husband has-beens,
much heave of gut about, for Henry diggin-

in, hooha, each syllable's a
laser at the
genitals.
But long and last, like much, it end.
We make ovation; stand to leave the hall.
Deep Henry sunk to hairtips lies, who gave an all.

And as they turn I see my couple:
man-face, woman-face the same; see they are
brother and sister. Brother, sister,
pair by pair we pass our way together,
into the arc of the dark beyond
the vestibule.

THE BLOOM OF AIR

for Judith

What was it you so liked to offer me?
A careful gift of nothing I could grasp.
An inch of space we traded solemnly,
Held forth in fingers newly learned to clasp.
I couldn't see for seeing, seeing I
Had taken views as dark as cataracts;
But you were small, and dwelling much less high
Than fathers do among apparent facts,
You charmed me to a traffic with the void,
A bloom of air we passed from hand to hand;
And if I gave it back best-half destroyed,
This essence I still hope to understand,
You turned it whole again; made up the waste.
Whatever I diminished, you replaced.

IN A STRANGER'S APARTMENT

I trespass through the silence as in shame,
and feel the mute persistence of her scent.
The way the soap lies tilted is her name;
the filter-tips she bit, books partly read,
the clock that stopped beside the unmade bed
as if it only wished to keep her time—
now everything's a relic: shoes seem meant;
a slip left hanging on the bathroom door
flows thinly down as if to pantomime
her absence; slants of light on tub and floor
hold motionless, long beams from blinds slit-eyed
that must have dazzled, crisscrossed, as she dried.

SWANS THEMSELVES

Evening spreads: a shadow of light
grown large on the water. Clear day is gone
that held to the mind a swan-reflection,
ravishing glass, mirror of calm.

But swans themselves: they pick at their feathers
like one-legged beggars against a wall;
or bully ducks by the scruff of the neck;
or sleep on the banks, connubial,
their heads tucked in tight
like unbaked loaves.

I've seen them walking the highway, leaving
their pastoral function, plodding, ungainly,
whitened by dusk:
priests, defrocked.

But once swans rose above me, lovely,
ah they were lovely in heavy beauty,
soaring, length of their bone-necks pointing,
Nordic ships bearing tons of body
silently with them:
outsailing night.

III
From
TEACHING
THE PENGUINS
TO FLY

NURSING HOME

My mother babbles. A salad of noises.
"You know who this is?" asks my aunt and I dread
some horror of an answer, but no,
nothing. She rubs her tray instead.
"It's clean," says my aunt, "the tray is clean.
Evelyn, what are you cleaning? Play
with your cards, play *pishy-posh*"—and then she
laughs, that overflowing, tilts
her head at the word and laughs who sits
all day in her chair with her cards in a sweater
embroidered with flowers, all day each day
where the t.v. flickers. My aunt thinks she chose
senility. My aunt says you have to keep
moving, never worry, avoid
abiding mourning,
things that refuse to change.

MY MOTHER'S CHILDHOOD

When she still used words, my mother told
of her childhood: they were poor, her father
peddled insurance door-to-door
in Portland, where the firehouse bell
would ring *no school* come heavy snow
and she'd stand—her little shrug, her sheepish
grin—in the candy factory yard,
waiting, patient child in the cold,
for sometimes an upper window would open,
someone would throw down gum, lumps
as large as little pumpernickels;
grey, but tasty. How she chewed!
She never wondered then, was it pure?
rejected?—chewed till her jawbones ached
and the tears welled in her eyes—they only
threw to her, to her, because
she waited,
and was good.

THE GIRL NOT INVITED

What will sweeten the life of the girl
not invited? There works a bitterness
yellow through gauze, an acid stench
no words diffuse, staining the cells
of her nature. What if everyone
were invited, say for a thousand years,
till even her lump's distinction, her lead-grained
silence leached away, and the starch
of pain had dimmed from the fiber? Who could
like her, want her, dustier all
the time and no damn fun and she hardly
blames them, the happy few, they need
the presence of an absence. She carries
her carapace, the weight of the self-
protected, but dreams she shatters the pear
and the Ford and Bonnie and Clyde and each round
hole through metal and flesh, each round-eyed
hole is splatting *me, me,* the word *me!*

THE EVIDENCE

My friends away, I feed their cats,
who lean against my legs, pass,
repass, mrrrr through a silence dense
as cold, unqualified cold, though this
is a summer day where I go my rounds
with the blue tin watering can, serving
the fiddleleaf ficus, the octopus tree.

Finished, oddly awed, the key
light in my hand on its poppit chain,
I pause, wait: above the clarified
kitchen sink, across the length
of linoleum, out beyond the lawn
in the meadow the purple loosestrife blazes,
ordered and mad at once, and I am

witness to the evidence
of choice: chairs; a napkin holder;
magazines that came and came;
notes held up by the phone with paint-chipped
magnets; yellow, blue, alphabet
letters on the fridge that spell
confusion in Finno-Ugric; children's

paintings tacked to the doors; rooms
a child no longer a child will remember—
clutter to bear familiar pain
to the heart: the smell of one's parents: photos
in silver frames on the polished dresser:
monogrammed backs of brushes: cuff links . . .
the unrelenting, historical air.

BORGES IN CAMBRIDGE

"You find this photo flatters me?
Too dark, I think. Too somber. I've sought
throughout my life the Jewish forebear
it's certain I must have. Ur-kafka.
Anything fondly willed may yield
a presence. On well-named Memorial Drive
we chant *The Wanderer* together,
hreran mid hondum hrimcealde sae . . .
I find myself in touch with camps
of the ancients, gone, familiar . . . distant
streets more real than these, hands . . .
you say the gift is *attention?* Exactly:
no more nor less
than a hunting cat's."

MY TEACHER

1

"Consider this pig," my teacher said.
"It grows so fat, it smells so bad,
it is perfect of its kind. You must
be brave, express the thoughts you've kept
hidden in your heart, whether joyous
or vile!"

I gave her a page smeared thick
with mud.

"Now this is fine," she said,
"a poem in praise of wind and bird
for their scattering of seed."

2

"I am like a man . . ." I began to explain.

"True," she said.

"But I yearn to become
a master, a survivor!"

"Too much
trying."

"I'll try not to try . . ."

"*Much* too much trying!"

3

"Consider yourself," she told me, "you wish
to be loved, admired, for fear of displeasing
you live an endless discipleship
wearing this mask with a grin, constant
but cold."

"It is my face," I said.

"May it melt in the sun," said my teacher.

TO A LADY

Dear lady, by your fingertips
you rhyme me to a feather.
I run the rapids of your arms
from here to Minnesota.
You sun me bright, you sigh me on
till half of Iceland's burning.
I bless you for your leafy ways.
My breath be all you're wearing.

IN THE FORTIES

you give up wasting your youth, move on
to the wasting of the rest. . . at times
you notice a sultry, weathered feeling,
as if your thoughts had spent a week
in a sherry cask, or your life's a house
where the unpainted shingles have darkened at last
from sea salt. Think "Gray is beautiful,"
and a strolling girl on the beach may give you
a look—something to do with her father?
his smile, his military brushes?—
that proves you're still yourself, for time
begins beyond your gates, another's
vision counts you down but not
your own: within, you're going for extra
bases, running towards waves, strolling
through sunlight, pigeons, traffic, anyone,
anyone you see
liable to change you.

TEACHING THE
PENGUINS TO FLY

The penguins must have had it once,
some drive and wingspan, back before
they joined up in committees to waddle
on slow-moving ice floes, flapping rhetorical
vans. My daughter's first ambition
was teaching them to fly, and she hasn't
forgotten: a poster of Emperor penguins
hangs on her bedroom wall where Beatles
still remain, and Aquarius,
her sign—the fuzzy young and vaguely
gazing adults, all of them look
like kids who've lost their expedition
leader. Emperors. Most of them show
color enough at the neck for the mythseeking
eye to propose, from vestigial yellows,
ancestor roc-macaws. Fifteen,
already the culture-heroine knows
it's nothing like easy to start them moving;
she'll leap and flap her arms to teach
the huge idea: up on the toes
higher, higher, lift those wings!—
trials down ice-slicked runways, lengthy
political sessions, building the Movement,
until the strongest risk the winter
sky, shedding their dickies, becoming
through generations enormous budgies
who sing in the jungle, in general bird,
the epic tale of the odd liberator
in shirt and jeans who beat the air
with her arms, who sang them
Woody Guthrie, who
brought the revolution
uncramping their lives.

THE OLD

At first it seems there's nobody
not old but you: the bully's 9 feet
tall, six, already goes
to school, oh he is ancient in
his cruelty; the parents live
forever; uncles let you watch
gin rummy, blitz, schneider, aunts
arrive with furs and gossip, cheeks
so lovely cool to kiss and you are
something else who'd understand
their pleasures—what a lesson, watching
Cousin Lou at twenty put
his feet up, trying not to grin
as he contemplates the first fine ash
of his White Owl! You have learned the names
of radio stations, KYW,
WFIL, the price
of an eighth of a pound of lox for breakfast
around the corner on Rockland Street,
but you think of the old as a species, speaking
pidgin to their hearing aids,
the ones who hobble, the ones who smile
to themselves, the ones who pee their pants,
and you by now a lover, father,
bowling with your son, having
your eyes examined, jogging your lungs
eight minutes every morning they're blurring
the changes of season you're getting Sup-hose
and a porkpie hat for Christmas, every
year through thicker glass until you're
moving toward a central light
from which the young are shadows: simply
flutter: less
than real.

IV
From
IMAGINING
A UNICORN

THE TIMES

My daughter tells me her dream, where she saw
The Times on the porch in the morning and knew
from the page-sized black of the headlines—WAR—
DECLARES WAR—that now it was over, and wept
in her dream to think that she'd never have
her years, friends, a marriage night,
shifting the dreck of everyday life...
a young woman mourning, telling her father
her dream, and he goes sadly in search
of rage, he's able at anything
but rage: he will stretch out his arm, his hand,
ashamed to see
how not a finger trembles.

WOMAN IN THE SUBWAY

Once in the subway a downcast woman
moved along the platform saying
"Talk to me? Talk to me?" No one replied.
Refusal—tight-lipped turning away—
seemed the world's oldest profession, so when she
reached me I spoke. "What?" I said,
and at once she lifted the word to her mouth
like a frog from the swamp: "Ra-*whaaat?*" she mocked,
turning in circles, blaring, as if
she'd won, she'd made someone speak, a fellow
human: "Ra-*whaat?* Ra-*whaat?*"

THE PALE ONES

A clearing: a burnt-out space: it was either
that, or they'd hack down altogether
the wilderness back of your eyes. So we scorched,
with the usual pain and help, the usual
square for such a case—you built
your hut with the wide veranda, achieved
the houseboy, all as it should be, the bottle
of Jameson, volumes of Wharton and Maugham,
the white goat at the fence, the shrub
at the well. Now drain your glass, now fold
your hands and nod to the sunset—nice.
Later the basic creatures will grunt
at the waterhole. But those that rushed
from the blaze at first, the shy amazing
pale ones, appearing
tottering, blinking
at your edges: have they gone
beyond? back in? are they hiding? At times
when you think you sleep, near dawn, I listen,
and softly, very softly, I hear you
call them.

LIKE THIS

In my box of a cinderblock office in Building
14, I doze on the narrow couch and you
haven't phoned and it strikes me that lying
dead will be packaged and cold and straight
like this, exactly like this, only minus
the clock you bought me, the books, the sketch
Caren sent from Rome—and yes, of course,
no window, no rising to watch a boy
and his dog below; but otherwise just
like death, only adding the chair the lamp the
chess column clipped from the Thursday *Times* and your
voice your laughter the wind on the way
to the car that claims it's real that says
it will slap my face awake or push me
down or twist me in half if it wants to.

ACROSS THE HALL

I hear you naming names, students,
Iris Dellums, Lois Ann
McCann: shadowy smiling faces
slide in a yearbook progress back
of my eyes. Reading names, setting
grades perhaps, preparing a list
by dictation, calling role: *Mary*
Rietz, Mimsi Bressler, Arbor
Helms. Saying them out, saying them
each one out in your poet's level
manner, each with an edge, a border
of pause, matte of dignity made
by your rhythm, tongue, bronze and watery
blade of words. Even as
you speak I'm mourning you, and me,
and *Muffy Brown.* Slow-moving passage.
Every week and year everywhere
officers preachers dictators foremen
name them name them *Anna Teplock*
Marnie Zimmer Barbara Pachman
bless the living bless the living
Celia Benjamin
Irma Jean O'Neil

SPACKS STREET

Fame: fame: whole generations
going up in pique, uncalled,
unchosen! Silly to waste much strength
earning a place of note (there's not
a grave without
its certified *has-been*)—
but once. . . I wanted a star in my name;
or a state, a river, a unit of measure. . .
a street, at least. . . Spacks Street. . . Spacks Place. . .
how nice! Imagine the little kids
playing Giant Steps after dinner in summer,
leaping from one of your curbs to the other.
Or someone moves, does well, gains weight
and years and accolades, and says
"God, if they only could see me today,
the old gang
back on Spacks Street!"

LIKE A PRISM

On any particular morning
the paunchy gent in the basement room,
not feeling like Sancho or Falstaff, is laughed at
by boys who see him, half awake,
through the grating, and know they'll never, ever,
look like that, bloated, sad,
pleased by nothing
but sleep . . . on a normal
morning in this world, while the new bride
slips away, excited, to count
her sheets still pampered in tissues, and many
die of the drought, or their color, or taste
in justice, there's something
we want will not
be given, we blessed
of the day—a bitter
dream curves down our mouths to a state
of iron—we need the password, exemption
from guilt and grief, for we are no longer
struck to learn that the torturer works
his wonders on any
particular morning.

We need for God himself to say
All right, all right to be fed, to take up
space on the planet, to
cherish the day, to
draw a share, like a prism,
of its light.

THE VENTNOR WATERWORKS

I was holding the phone, desperate, you know,
—the burnt-out coil, the warranty refund—
waiting to scream at the claims adjuster

when out of the past a chill green pleasure
rose through my body: summers riding
my bike to the Ventnor Waterworks
to drink from the cold of its fountain. I'd enter

as if at a temple: no human sound:
ferns, everywhere ferns and a passionate
coolness—and here I am, thirty years later,

shouting like any maniac,
steward of sour grapes, "I want
my car! That's not my problem, I want
my car!"

COUNTING THE LOSSES

for Helen Corsa

Yeats, who mourned youth's sweetness gone
  All that is lost is the body
slept, he said, on boards, to turn
his verses hard, and hardened sung
solace for the ox-eyed, stunned
animal of desire. Rossini,
shocked by his mother's death, gave over
music with its grandeur, became
a chef—a sort of mother—seeking
to yield the milk of consolation.
Goya, beauty's nightmare lover,
mad from leadwhite, vicious war,
saw his duchess, named for dawn,
in the form of a toad, in the yellow gloom
of a circus, sickly, running down;
he painted children with massive heads,
a giant bestriding a hillside; etched
a chicken plucked alive by fiends
  All that is lost is the body.

Approaching composition the laureate
  All that is lost is the body.
said and resaid his name like the clack
of British Railways: *Tennyson,*
Tennyson-Tennyson, murmuring
of innumerable *be's*—mere being,
humiliating history.
Heinrich Schleimann, final hero
of Troy, saw as a child a tombstone:
"here lies Heinrich Schliemann"—(a brother,

dead in infancy)—"Beloved
Son" *himself! in the grave!* He told
lies to the Turks, would have killed to continue
digging for Helen's balconies,
for Priam's gate; a lifetime, raising
the other from the dead. That all
we suffer be raised and opened, that
is our portion, work, to lift from the grave—
he who digs is the living son

All that is lost is the body.

IMAGINING A UNICORN

AFTER THE UNICORN TAPESTRIES AT THE CLOISTERS

Theoretically, there exists a perfect possibility of happiness:
to believe in the indestructible element in oneself and not strive
after it.—Kafka, Parables and Paradoxes

1

With greyhounds and with running hounds
You gather to hunt the unicorn,
Grave seignors in the flowery field—
Spirit that leaps with earthweight on,
Noble spirit, white as the wind—
You seek his trail with spears in hand,
"That furious beast, His precious horne"
Turning to dove-song every poison,
Asp of envy, kiss of assassin.
"The greatness of his mynde is such
He chooseth rather to dye than be taken."

•

White, whole-of-the-spectrum white,
Come from afar, like starlight,
He kneels beside the sullied waters,
Drawing the venom into himself
While lion and leopard, stinking hyena,
Wait to drink. He dips his horn,
Noblesse oblige; untouchably bright.
The peacock meets his face in the fountain.
The hunters wait until he leaps:
Law of the chase. That others may drink:
Charity, in an animal dream!

•

He rushes on, quarry of kings:
By walnut, linden, trembling aspen,

Periwinkle, "joy of the ground,"
Forget-me-nots of Mary's color.
Takes to the stream; defends himself.
A dog's impaled, aie! aie!
Water-, wind-, fireheart-white:
By hawkweed, bluebell, primrose, clary,
Speared, surrounded—untamable—
And yet he enters the rose-wound fence,
The virgin's thorn-crowned loveliness.

2

For passion we seek you, goat-chinned horse,
Lover and teacher, feral Christ:
Holy body that never lies;
Among us as long as we think you are—
By orange tree, madonna lily,
Always the maiden's one intended,
Cragpacer, dog-killer, furious source
For those who wove your tapestry,
Spinning your rosebuds out of the worm
And thistles saying "Mary," "Mary"—
Rapt-eyed image of charity.

•

Among the partridges, plump as lust,
Christ, little buket, whatever your name,
Held by a woman's gentle touch,
Now you are ready to take your death,
Spirit that draws its earthweight on;
More than us yet close to us,

Soul that enters its earthly home
Amid the oak, the beech, the palm,
Pattern of beauty's brilliance, strangeness;
Beauty of violence; beauty of calm;
This flood: this sleep: these marriages.

●

Noblesse oblige: ready for death
As her handmaiden waves the spearsmen in.
Called to his death, mysterious,
By the horn of the hunter Gabriel.
Bowing down, bowing down, though fully strong,
To the salted wounds of sacrifice:
Spear in the neck, spear in the side
—Only we would seek to destroy him,
We in our terror of worthlessness—
Dogs on his back: substantial God;
Torn by the world; rose-touched; dead.

3

They bear the corpse to the royal city,
And there a little boy turns away,
Petting his dog: will not look, for sorrow.
And there a lady turns away,
Seeing the bridegroom wreathed with thorn,
On trodden flowers heavily borne.
Nightingale in the medlar bush,
Squirrel in the hawthorne boughs obscured,
Little city with bannerettes,
Coopers and cooks, saddlers and gossips—
This sadness, over and over again.

•

Are you still in our world, great unicorn?
You who drew the rage of men
Into you like a poison—returned,
Always renewed, a gift to us,
—Plenitude upon plenitude—
Curing our wants with fruits and flowers,
Who kill as a charm for deathlessness.
You who have bled, your wounds are gone,
The blood you shed from the vicious hunt
Juice of love-apple, staining your coat,
O holy body that never lies!

•

Hunters, your greed would drink his strength—
See, he returns; his wounds are gone.
Princely, forgiving, unendingly born,
He marries the garden of the earth,
Plenitude upon plenitude;
The cuckoopint and paquerette:
Butterfly, bittern, gnat, civet—
Frog and bee and startled rabbit—
Plenitude, plenitude!—wild strawberry:
Duck and dog and feverfew:
Daisy—day's eye—sun as a flower;

The hazeltree, and the holly.

MALEDICTION

You who dump the beer cans in the lake;
who in the strict woods sow
the bulbous polyethylene retorts;
who from your farting car
with spiffy rear-suspension toss
your tissues, mustard-steaked, upon
the generating moss; who drop
the squamules of your reckless play,
grease-wrappers, unspare parts, lie-labeled
cultures even flies would scorn
to spawn on—total Zed, my kinsman
ass-on-wheels, my blare-bred bray
and burden,
               may the nice crabs thread
your private wilds with turnpikes; weasels'
condoms squish between your toes,
and plastic-coated toads squat *plop*
upon your morning egg—may gars
come nudge you from your inner-tube,
perch hiss you to the bottom, junked,
a discard, your dense self your last
enormity.

GERARD

for Nicole Pinsky

The easels went to the swift, namely
Irving Berman and me, back
when I was in kindergarten, Nicole.
Two easels, so we raced, come arts
& crafts. I usually won, am strange
about winning yet: sometimes even
hang back a bit who early shoved
my way, intense to make it, first
to get there first, and only then
to love the giant bottles of yellow
and blue and schloshing around on the paper
various genius items, and all
this while Gerard would sit in his corner:
he always accepted the banging-sticks
in the orchestra, the rest of us calling
"Me! Me!" for the glockenspiel;
Gerard the heavily mothered, lost
the first day, tearful, beating the door,
his mother gone and couldn't hear him
no matter how hard he cried, as teacher
explained, and next day the same, what luscious
sport, Gerard with his oval head
and museum guard demeanor, convenient
Gerard—forced to wear rubbers, galoshes,
black floppers every day, and every
day a man's black umbrella, imagine,
even in breathless June, grim
Mr. Junior Death Gerard with shame
on his feet, above his head, we almost
died, Lenny and Irving and Wilma
and Neil and Shirley and Marvin and me:
wizened Gerard, saved from the rain—
Gerard, Gerard, we called your name
till you wept: that hushed us a bit, and then:

> Gerard, Gerard
> Momma's pet!
> Gerard, Gerard,
> Don't get wet!

(Am I telling you this for forgiveness, Nicole?
I hear at your kindergarten you flinch
at the sudden shrill of the schoolyard bell;
can't bear the noise and confusion; it's good
your teacher lets you in before
the rest, but please, if they start to shout

> Nicole, Nicole,
> Jump in a hole!

or other stuff like that, will you kindly
let us know, and we'll fix it up
somehow, we lords of creation?)—meanwhile
Gerard's a judge by now I'd guess,
or a millionaire, or both, with regular
habits—or what if he turned out folksy,
Just Plain Bill, why not? or a hairy
prophet, a poet, a singing waiter,
anything, engineer or enter-
tainer, amazement to wife and kids
and friends, no permanent damage—but oh
Come back Gerard, and we'll take off your rubbers,
we'll fracture that damned umbrella in 12,000
pieces, we'll lock your mother in
the room with the little chairs, we'll lift you
shoulder high, home to our ethnic
slovenly moms and pops who'll feed you
kasha with bowties, *flanken* and gravy,
and let you stay up, *on a school night,* for Mr.
Keen, Gang Busters, Norman Corwin
Presents, and pack you off next day
happy, straight through the pouring rain.

V

NEW POEMS

THE THOUGHT OF LIGHT

We were the summer's witnesses,
Charmed by the bright impertinence
Of strolling evenings, cape and cane.

We spread our toes in our good mud
When all this spoil of shadowed field
Grew lush with clover's rich obliging.

Deep in the house the thought of light
Still moves the leaves of all our plants
To turn, cell after cell, near dawn.

Improving their greens and shapeliness
They face the not yet risen sun—
As we did when we turned to kiss

Who slog through winter like a war.

THE DOWNRIGHT POET

Grim Story

The Downright Poet polluted his wine
set fire to his house
drove his pigs to the sea

so at once became hungry, thirsty, needy
of shelter. How did he
carry on?

In open air.
Drinking living gall.
Eating his hopeful heart out.

Definition

Man is a freestanding solitude
—so the Downright Poet definded him, sad,
out where the Goths and the Ostrogoths
will never stoop to find him. "Man
is an unfeathered, two-legged, love-making creature
digging and poisoning wells."

His Scholarship

The D.P. was born in the usual way,
parade-rest stance, damp and bawling,
eyes and needs and a sexual organ.
Do better men have better dreams?
He woke to a grimmer whim each day—
till he reached for an interest in most things great
and small, as Coleridge advises, snakes
and waterbugs and the albatross
plus the Matrons of Winnetka, noting
82 species of Matron: the *Whiner,*
Shouter, Whisperer, Smiler, Weeper . . .
and manfully entered on scholarship.

The No-Nonsense Surgeon

"What is art, after all?" asked the No-Nonsense Surgeon,
pausing, his hands full of dripping guts.
"I mean, does it void the pancreas?
will it aliment the phagocytes?
Is it flipflop Open Heart Surgery?
Finished!" he cried, restuffing the patient.
The interns applauded, the bells rang out,
the nurses rose and fell in a body;
the No-Nonsense Surgeon bowed left and right
(curtain call, curtain call!)
and cleaved the next in line. "I know,"
he whispered to the D.P. slyly,
"we've all got a touch of the poet."

Ambition

Sometimes the D.P.'s falling-down mad—
he'd have more fun as the Downright Flycatcher!
or Downright *God*. . .now say, what *about* that—
applying, not pausing for reverent airs:
"Have You thought at all about early retirement?
Open the job to younger talent?"
But gets no response. No bushes burn.
No tablets stack up at his feet.

What's Laughable

Many, he knows, hardly see the joke,
contrariness and brouhaha. . .
if they laugh once a month that's a major event
like sex before lunch or a sneeze at a concert,
but in his heart he'll hang his head:
always for him much is laughable,
namely Himself, and Others.

LIVING SIMPLY

Plato and Aristotle were well-bred men, and like others, laughing with their friends: and when they diverted themselves in making their laws and politics they did it playfully. It was the least philosophical and least serious part of their lives. The most philosophic was living simply and tranquilly.—Pascal, *Pensées*

Humans seem lonely even while dancing.
We tighten ourselves like the pain of a razor,
sigh like a mourner passing through.
The letter "I," frail thinking reed,
will loom like a column blocking our view
but whatever we say the day will continue,
the grasshoppers sing to the provident ants.

Mist at the delta...the breath's long river...
I'd take it on, neither host nor guest,
live out the wind like a battered flag.
No stillness has served to lengthen my shadow,
no striving redeemed me, no purpose to please.
Rapt in the seedlight of the darkness
the world is braille...I finger my way.

I'm learning to name my sadness right,
that greed persists with nothing lacking.
I study to grasp the Yiddish of it,
this heavy surge of will and woe.
Though I enter the room where the silence is
with piccolos on the brain,
neither grass nor trees will be interrupted.

Breath of the mind that clouds the mirror,
gust in my heart; sweep the wide floor
of my countinghouse. From death and static
a music tunes in loud and clear
and everything's real, weddings and Bangkok.
I'd been here all along yet still
kept hoping to arrive.

THE POETRY BUG

Have your students really caught the poetry bug?
—Paper on Writing Class Evaluation at MIT

If, driving home from the Russian poet's
reading—he reads like a Russian, flailing
eyes and arms, thus making the women
listening, so they afterwards claim,
want to run unclothed in the snow—she flails
an arm as she steers along icy roads
crooning out loud in a kind of mock-Russian,
she's probably caught it; but if, as she drives,
she's jotting down notes with a Big Blue Marker,
her poem about the Russian ("Take me,
Voznesensky") at 30 miles
per hour to top a rise and see
a white-faced man in an orange parka,
mittened, waving her down, and seven
cars spread round at angles all over
the road, and applying the brakes while praying
they'll somehow hold—sliding, pumping,
steering into the skid—she's thinking
of how this image of losing oneself
at last in the hands of Chance as to hitting
or coasting to a stop might actually
fit in her Russian-poet poem
(or maybe better the one about easing
her laden mind into sleep) you *know*
your student has caught the poetry bug.

POEM FOR A PAINTER

for J.E.S.

As a lens, focused scrupulously,
Will seem to disappear,
Studying faces of friends
You strive to see
Only and exactly
What is there.

The high, suave lilacs,
The green of leaf and lawn,
No mystery subverts them,
No scene from a movie.
Transparent, you burn away
All mist of moony atmosphere.

And the charm returns, more grave,
Drawn through the hard
Devotion of your stare.
So the camel emerges, ghostly,
From the needle's eye,
Ambling on to heaven.

BABIES

They couldn't make out what she wanted, so much
in a hurry and having no English she raised
her voice the cashier warned her she shouted they
called the cops, eight days she screamed
in the psycho ward the same screams over
and over until a Spanish-speaking
nurse appeared:
                   she'd *left them, run out*
for milk and bananas, locked them in,
her babies, her babies
                       —that's what she's saying.
That's what she'll never stop
trying to say.

THE SEA

I wanted to look at the sea for once
as simple, peaceful: thought to forget
its seethe of plunder and pain, to declare it
only huge and green, to slide
the watered silk of its weaving surface,
snakeskin sea. And I came upon birds
with oil-clogged feathers, hunched in the sand:
they die in a stupor of dryness or lurch
their way toward the water weighted with tar
in a kind of suicide, returning
with plummage forever defiled. I'd planned
to pulse with the sleepy beat of the waves
that rise to hover, surge to sigh,
foam in a skitter racing the beach,
a new beach smoothened every day,
sands rearranged, foot- and paw-prints
gone, the tide's brown scrawl redrawn...

but the sea kept battering, will upon will,
innocent and horrible,
coming and coming again.

REGARDING CATS

1

In the beginning all was fur,
shapeless, without a flea, and the Maker
twitched Her whiskers and called it good,
but the evening and the morning and the second day,

seeing no signs of pounce or stretch
She became depressed: very dull, very dull,
this fur without tail or claw that never
yawned nor washed...and then She thought:

"Out of such firmament, pure fur-dust,
I will shape (in a form like Myself) My creature!"
And so came to be
the essential *us*.

2

A man fell in love with his cat. He prayed
to Aphrodite. The goddess heard,
changing the cat to a lovely woman
of excellent slimness, wit and grace.

However...upon their marriage night
a mouse (was it shoved by the goddess?) skittered
across the smooth parquet and the bride
leapt from the bed to the chase.

3

This cat I live with runs on tracks of silk.
It's clear I'm meant to smooth her till she purrs.
She drowses in the sun. I pour her milk.
Little she finds in nature isn't hers.

GLORY LEARNT FROM ROSES

One time she gave me roses,
Such purely overcome
Infatuated roses, fierce
But delicate their bloom,

That I who'd balked at yielding
To keep my spirit free
Aspired to strive like roses—
To live less meagerly.

I'd understood her roses:
Extravagance they meant—
And grew myself full-hearted
Studying their scent.

As petals fell I studied
To make autumnal sense;
Observed that slowest raining:
A thousand weigh an ounce.

She'd sent a gift of roses
And roses told me all:
How past their will they open,
How past their will they fall.

That's glory learnt from roses,
Whatever weight of hurt
Is bound to follow after
The blooming of the heart.

SONG: AFTER THE PARTY

The crippled thought
Of peopled rooms.
Lie straight till morning pales the sheet.

The tides of human froth. The dooms
Of luck or loss
That lips repeat.

The fear-formed smile that one must treat
As gaiety. The crying need.
The limping wish. The sheep-clothed greed.

And truth's defeat. And love's defeat.
Lie straight till morning pales the sheet.
Lie straight till morning pales the sheet.

THE SHAVER

From my father-in-law—jaunty at eighty,
sharp till the night of his death as to costs
and gossip, quips and profit—came
a box in the mail with clothes I'd never
wear: his pressed pajamas, hat
with a cocky feather bought too late
to flaunt in the open air. A man
of triumphs, mainly, everything neat,
he found himself a bargain rate
for his funeral, and joked about clinching
the sale—Poppa, you kept coming on!
My thanks for these relics, fastidious gifts
to a slovenly son-in-law who shared
your size. There's one I'll keep (not socks,
not carefully folded B.V.D.s
that gave me a touch of the horrors): your hand-
wound watch, whose Roman face displays
the sum of the passing days, what we have
in common—you with your neat white hair
and me, swarthy, clicking open
your shaver, white dust
in the holding chamber
I blow to the sink, your living stubble
that every strength of my being would keep
from my mouth and throat and nose.

AFTER STORM

By the river
where we went under
our spirits stroll
hand in hand—
through the tall grass by the river
where our bodies lost each other,
down the long banks of the river
where we drowned
broken and rushing
like branches after storm,
helpless and swirling
branches in the river.

A MARRIAGE

Clear now
of our long struggle
I can hear your voice, its strength
the sweet coldness
of river water.

And I can see you
as in the photograph
with your father and sister,
tall pretty girl,
pigtailed and freckled,

led, misled,
until you doubted
your beauty, body,
that you were one among us,
a person, like any other.

And, given distance,
I think of you
becoming smaller,
but cheerful, the way
the old are

with short white hair
and an easiness
you'd never know before,
and me, incredibly,
not there.

JUDGES IN SUMMER

Sometimes people who judge and judge
turn lovely in summer, with gin & tonics.

They shop at little roadside stands;
brood in a trance over silks of corn.

Lounging around, still starched from swimming,
they speak mild words in the evening air

and leave the work of keeping up standards
to bickering children, questions of worth

to the waves. In town, in handkerchief dresses,
rumpled white suits, they smile, they visit—

they water the garden; hum with the cat.
In shirt and jeans they climb the rocks

with wine in a thermos, a bag of bread
to throw to those ravenous muscles the gulls—

and there they offer a round of applause
(of the gentle sort once used watching tennis)

to see the fat sun dip away
through its showy orange time.

SIX SMALL SONGS
FOR A SILVER FLUTE

1

I know your secret, now I've caught you
With eyes wide open and lips asleep.

Parts of your body
Nap by turns.

A little finger.
A rib. A breast.

It only seems
You never drowse—

That there's always something
You're thinking to tell me.

2

Each sungold hair
On your forearm wants

Particular love, attended to
Not as amongst all the orphan children

But for herself—
Wants patient lips

To choose her, read her
Her bedtime story.

3

The book in your hand
Explains your life

As best it can.
You're touched. You write it

Friendly notes
In the margins.

4

A new French blouse . . .
Essentially . . . sleeves.

In it you are
The full flute-theme

Of the moon's
Favorite concerto.

5

The plastic ferns that smelled so bad
We put them out at the curb, hoping

Someone might steal them
Or bite their clothes off

Are back. They want a second chance.
Should I let them in? They say they've taken

Vows, that in this next life
They'll be wheat.

6

The more I think
How you walk through the rain

To gather herbs, the thoughtfuller
I get. I know some other songs

But they're all about men, somewhat out of tune,
For kettledrum, and bassoon.

THE 4 A.M. NEWS

Up before dawn on a greyblue morning
I think of my mother's Uncle Max
who shared my room when I was twelve.
I'd wake, he'd be reading *The Lives of the Saints,*
post-nightmare. "They're too good to be true.'"
What he loved, as a non-reconstructed Jew,
was their saintly patience and cunning; mad
denial of pain drew his scorn: he knew
the screams that tell when the barbs plunge in,
the groans of the charred on the grille. All night,
in the dark of himself, he'd been dreaming again
of helping the Nazis: buckets of teeth
to lug; brains, each stuck to burlap . . .
my gentle Greatuncle, chatting with me,
avoiding the 4 A.M. news.

THE WARM CONNECTION

Lost in sadness in this sad world
you scarcely know where you leave off
and other woe begins . . . as if
you were weeping underwater.

         Your friends,
concerned, approach to search your life
like blind men with an elephant,
and though there's little they get straight—
"A wall!" "A tree!" "A rope!"—it flows
from just such clumsy touch, the warm
connection, no more wooed by will
than God's grace in the hymnal, no more
sane . . .

         or you're in Arab heaven—
drowsing, fig trees, wine-bearing boys—
feeling your lightened troubles rise
like fallen angels returning. The sun
arrives, arrives, you're ever-ready,

but what if they all came close, your people?
turned real, intent to warm you through?

How many could you bear, as selves,
with hands and lips and eyes?

IRIS

Iris, your purple and mauve-purple swerves and wells,
your interstitial plumes, frail, fingercurved,
the thrust of borning-green in stem and spear,
have moved me now to practice speech again,
through words have often crowded out my light.
Yet once no shadow dims my sense of you,
what need to try to name your loveliness,
to speak your poise by ruffles, or in flames
your vulval tongues of yellow and dark yellow?
In threenesses you rise, unmoved, intent;
your royal cups ease open, all aflair.
And I must rise to join you with my words,
which are for me my yellows and dark yellows.

THINKING OF PEAS

for Tanya Berry

I think of peas slow-breathingly
Snug in the sleeper's heat of their pods,
Sensing the dawn through pallid selves;
Deep jade to pearl, the one green smell.

Here on a tableful of peas
Some pods hold homey families
Close in a country kitchen, down
To earth as toes shoe-tight; more rarely

Two alone, either end of the table,
Not speaking, in crystal splendor. I study
A fleur-de-lis pea-tree, magnificent,
Exposed in half of its pod; I lift

A single sphere between thumb and finger,
Fullgrown, wishing to sense its structure
(Under the delicate bloom of skin
Split, of course, and hard as bone).

The emptied pods, raised to the light,
Still show the shapes of all their clan;
They're marked with flecks, pale hieroglyphs
—How nature's fierce to pack things in!

With perfect parents, seamed to fit,
Peas loll. They're schoolmates on a chaise;
They're standers-in-line, waiting patiently
For some wonderful door to open.

NEILSEN

"They called me Battling Nelson," said Neilsen,
my neighbor. "Assumed I was Irish . . . fought
my way to school and back, plus home
for lunch—there's something I can't understand!"
(Somebody's parking a car at his curb)—
"What do they think, they live in my house?"
Or he's up on the roof, age 76,
brooming away the snow. "Insane,"
my daughter says, "it insulates."
We shrug, we both say: "Neilsen"—Neilsen's
throwing a stone at a dog, it's not
his dog, why use his tree?—each fall
he clears the leaves to his very boundary,
exact. I guess that all along
with his passion for neatness and property
he'd wanted only this: "O world,
MAKE SENSE!" "You boys! Get off that wall!
Is that your wall? is that your wall?"

ESSENCE

A hummingbird taps at my window, stirred
By reflected lilacs, seductively blurred
In the glass. Astray from
An actual blossom
He'll yearn for this other
Spirit-flower,
Mirrored beauty
Surpassing sense;
Idea only;
Ache of romance.

EVENING SONG

Stars with their thoughtful faces
Burn atoms the size of a town,
While cells in acute mathematics
Like planets roll around.

A thought made of earth, I labor
To see the dim world through the film
I've screened all my life for its drama
From my narrow projection room.

The day keeps entering darkness
Through the wide door of the dusk
While I, alone with my changes,
Move with the sun toward the west.

Whatever endures beyond breathing
I yield myself to its care,
That floods day and night past believing,
That hums with no need that I hear.

POEM

Will it come again like this?
Will we ever get it right?
It is always as it is,
And it passes.

Never as it was,
Yet always somehow bright,
Always somehow sweet
In its changes.

We will never get it right.
It will come, but not like this.
It is always as it is,
And it changes.

A teacher of writing and literature for many years at the Massachusetts Institute of Technology and a visiting professor at other universities, Barry Spacks has published four previous collections of poems: *The Company of Children, Something Human, Teaching the Penguins to Fly,* and *Imagining a Unicorn.* He is also an actor and the author of two novels, *Orphans* and *The Sophmore.*

THE JOHNS HOPKINS UNIVERSITY PRESS

SPACKS STREET: *New & Selected Poems*

This book was composed in Galliard text and display type by Brushwood Graphics, from a design by Susan P. Fillion. It was printed on S. D. Warrens's Sebago Eggshell paper and bound in Kivar 5 by Universal Lithographers, Inc.

Many of the poems in *SPACKS STREET* appeared in the following volumes: *THE COMPANY OF CHILDREN*, by permission of Doubleday and Co.; *SOMETHING HUMAN*, by permission of Harper and Row; *TEACHING THE PENGUINS TO FLY*, by permission of David R. Godine, Publisher, Inc.; *IMAGINING A UNICORN*, by permission of The University of Georgia Press.

Previously published poems originally appeared in the following periodicals, some in slightly different form:
ANTAEUS: *The Vireo; Songs from a Cook Book*
ATLANTIC MONTHLY: *The Pale Ones*   BELOIT
POETRY JOURNAL: *Day Full of Gulls; Swans Themselves*
BOSTON MAGAZINE: *The Abstract Notion of Boston, Gathering Dust*   CALIFORNIA QUARTERLY: *Thinking of Peas*   CAN: *Exercises*   CARLETON
MISCELLANY: *The Strolling Crow*   COLLEGE
ENGLISH: *Across the Hall*   COUNTER/MEASURES: *The Bloom of Air*   CUMBERLAND POETRY REVIEW: *Poem for a Painter*   EQUAL-TIME: *Shaving*
ESQUIRE: *My Teacher*   GEORGIA REVIEW: *Spacks Street; Babies*   HARPER'S MAGAZINE: *Like This*
HUDSON REVIEW: *Teaching the Penguins to Fly; Woman in a Subway; Neilsen; Essence*   LITTLE SQUARE
REVIEW: *Songs from a Cook Book*   MASSACHUSETTS
REVIEW: *The Ventnor Waterworks*   NATION: *At 35*   NEW YORKER: *Freshmen; The Outrageously Blessed; Like a Prism; The Shaver; The Warm Connection*   NEW
YORK TIMES: *Themes on Love; Emblems for Lovers; To a Lady*   NOBLE SAVAGE: *The World as a Vision of the Unity in Flesh*   PLACE: *Gerard*   PLOUGHSHARES: *Nursing Home; The Times; Counting the Losses*
POETRY: *Recommendations; Imagining a Unicorn; Malediction; Living Simply; The Poetry Bug; Judges in Summer*
POETRY NORTHWEST: *Poem*   QUARTERLY WEST: *The 4 A.M. News*   RADIX: *In a Stranger's Apartment*
SEWANEE REVIEW: *My Clothes; The Thought of Light; Glory Learnt from Roses; Song: After the Party*